BIG WORDS FOR LITTLE PEOPLE

Helen Mortimer & Cristina Trapanese

Celebrate

FESTIVAL

Kane Miller
A DIVISION OF EDC PUBLISHING

Milestones

As we grow up, we are always reaching milestones. It feels good to celebrate them.

Birthdays

Cards, good wishes, and cake!

Happy birthday!

These are just some of the ways to mark the day you were born.

Up on your feet

We love to celebrate by dancing.

Music

We sing and play instruments
to mark happy times.

Traditions

We can keep our folktales, myths, and legends alive by telling each other stories.

Food

A special occasion almost always includes food! When we share favorite dishes, we discover new tastes.

Try one of these!

Words, words, words

There are many different greetings for any celebration. Here are some words you'll often hear.

THREE CHEERS!

HAPPY ...

MERRY ...

CONGRATULATIONS!

LET'S PARTY!

WELCOME!

WISHING YOU ...

HIP, HIP, HOORAY!

YOU'VE WON!

WELL DONE!

Color

From carnival costumes to kites,
from fairy lights to fireworks,
when we celebrate, color
is everywhere!

Favorite things

There are lots of things we like to do,
which we can celebrate with each other.

What do you love?

SCIENCE TENT
BOOK CORNER
PAINTING SHED
NATURE DEN
GO BANANAS!

Something new

A new baby, a new home, a new skill,
a new tooth!

New friend!

Each one deserves
a celebration.

Each other

It feels good when we come together for happy and even sad times. Whether there are tears or smiles, each one is special and brings everyone closer.

Celebrate

Celebrate being you, celebrate
what you can do, celebrate
special days, celebrate every day!

Ten ideas for getting the most from this book

1 Take your time. Sharing a book gives you a precious chance to experience something together and provides so many things to talk about.

2 This book is all about how we celebrate. What celebrations do you have coming up on your family calendar?

3 It's also a book about language. What words can we use to help someone celebrate any special occasion?

4 The illustrations in this book capture various moments on a visit to a winter street festival. Why not suggest what might have happened just before each moment and what might happen next?

5 We've intentionally not given the children names—so that you can choose your own and perhaps invent something about their personalities. What name would you give the little dog?

Otis?

Peanut?

Princess?

Ozzy?

6 As well as celebrating big, important events, we should constantly celebrate things that matter to us: our achievements, our families, our friends, our passions, and ourselves. Has anything happened in your day today to celebrate?

7 Think about an imaginary celebration! What food and games would you have at a party for an alien, or a unicorn, or a shark, or a pixie?

8 Why not make a family box for celebration keepsakes? It could be a place to keep all sorts of things like invitations, cards, pictures, and certificates. You could decorate it with lots of jazzy, celebratory patterns and colors.

9 By exploring the ways in which we can mark and share any special occasion, we hope this book will give children and the adults in their lives the tools they need to express themselves and take part in the world around them.

10 You could each choose a favorite word about celebrating from the book—it will probably be different each time you share the story!

Glossary

folktales – stories which are remembered by people telling them to each other

mark – if we mark something, we celebrate an event in a special way

milestone – an important step or event

myths and legends – traditional stories